The Art of Small Talk & Winning First Impressions

How to Start Conversations, Build Rapport and Have Relationships That Last!

By Ric Phillips, MBA

The Art of Small Talk & Winning First Impressions –

How to Start Conversations, Build Rapport and Have Relationships That Last!

INTRODUCTION

Welcome to the next level of your interpersonal communication skills training!

The philosophy of this book is to provide you with the theory and practical application of the most used and therefore essential communication skills needed in making a great first impression and then starting meaningful and memorable conversations. Will we cover all the relevant communication skills? I don't think it's possible, but since effective communication is a pillar of personal and business success, we will cover the most essential points for sure. It will hopefully not only give you tools and techniques to use right away but also get you thinking about what other communication skills might be valuable to you as you aim to build your professional and social networks. I encourage you to seek out new ways to continue to grow your communication skills understanding and implementation in business and your social life.

In early 2006 I started a communication coaching and training company called 3V Communications. You might be curious about that name. It is important that we recognize the distinct advantage we have when we can communicate with confidence and clarity using the 3Vs of communication. So, what are they?

The 3V's are Verbal (our words, phrases, grammar, slang etc.), Vocal (our rhythm, speed, volume, intonation etc.) and Visual (body language, gestures, attire, accessories, environment, etc.). Our goal is to align or synchronize these 3Vs to produce an intentional 4th V – your VIBE.

My personal and professional mission is very clear: "to empower you and open doors to social and professional opportunities by enhancing your skills and knowledge in key areas of communication." It is my goal to assist all kinds of people in this important area of communication, whether they are from this country or another, man or woman, young or old, outgoing or shy. We all can benefit from better communication skills.

I would like to thank my family and friends, specifically those that empower and support me in my endeavours and adventures. You know who you are.

I would like to thank my clients, for without whom I would have not have a business with which to try to better myself!

Finally, I would like to thank the authors and businesspeople that have taken the time to compile research and present their information to the public, so that we may benefit from their knowledge. I have learned so much and continue to learn from many diverse people, most of whom I have never met.

Perhaps now it is my turn (in my own small way) to give back to society with this book. To your success!

Ric Phillips

ABOUT THE AUTHOR

Ric Phillips, MBA – Ranked in Top 30 'Communication Professional' by

Global Gurus since 2022!

In a nutshell Ric Phillips has been studying human communication all his life, and teaching communication skills professionally since 1998, here and abroad. Ric understands the damage caused by miscommunication or worse yet, by boring, non- persuasive communication. He believes there is no reason to accept generic or below-par corporate communications in today's modern world.

Mr. Phillips studied sociology & psychology at university and later completed his MBA. After gaining hands-on experience with social work and then high-level customer service in the office world of finance, he decided to teach ESL abroad, accepting a post at a Chinese teacher's college for 2 years. After returning to

Toronto Ric transferred his love of teaching communicative English to focus on business English skills, and in 2002 started teaching business communication skills and accent reduction to immigrant professionals in Toronto/GTA.

Through practical work and study Ric expanded his repertoire and became Canada's first Communication Coach in 2006, inspired to teach others to master the unique holistic system he had understood – the 3Vs of communication - the Verbal, the Vocal and the Visual. Ric became a certified Coach and NLP (Neuro-Linguistic Programming) practitioner, and body language expert. With his formal education, his many years of teaching and his innate understanding of human behaviour Ric founded 3V Communications Ltd. in 2007. Through 3V Ric coaches entrepreneurs, executives, managers and staff, and creates highly interactive communication workshops for companies both here and abroad. 3V also creates industry-specific communication assessments for organizations that help evaluate candidates for recruiting and training purposes.

Since 2013 he has been a Program Advisor & Instructor of business communication skills for YEDI – York Entrepreneurship Development Institute, where his main purpose is to train entrepreneurs how to communicate their brand, network effectively, pitch their venture, and use effective interpersonal and professional communications in business and life. He is now senior staff.

In 2016 Ric spearheaded the creation of the nationally registered non-profit organization NCCA

(National Communication Coaching Association of) Canada. He put together a strong Board and leads the team as Executive Director.

Ric is a frequent conference speaker, a TEDx speaker, and has trained communication skills in outside of Canada in China, Russia, Armenia, Israel, France, Japan and the USA.

As an author of ebooks, articles and a blog since 2006, and a co-author of the 2024 book "Pinnacle of Influence, How the World's Greatest Thought Leaders Became Global Gurus", Ric is an expert in communications, public speaking techniques and body language analysis, frequently called upon by media to provide pundit opinion and advice on businesspeople, politicians and celebrities. He gave such analysis regarding the Canadian federal elections, the Ontario provincial leadership debates, Lance Armstrong's interview with Oprah, Toronto Mayor Rob Ford's media apologies and interactions, Donald Trumps' handshakes, the cultural body language gestures of Asia, and a variety of professional communication strategies for the North American office.

More about Ric can be found at:

https://www.linkedin.com/in/communicationcoach

TEDx Talk: https://www.youtube.com/watch?v=SuG-BHquAHU Amazon Author Page: https://www.amazon.com/Ric-Phillips/e/B071L861J8 YouTube Channel:

https://www.youtube.com/@RicPhillips

ISBN: 979-8-89795-837-5

All reasonable attempts have been made to verify the accuracy of the information provided in this publication. Nevertheless, the author assumes no responsibility for any errors and/or omissions.

The opinions expressed within this book and on the websites are those of the author and authors of other resources and should not be considered legal or professional advice. This book has been produced for educational purposes only, not to be utilized solely or in lieu of a consultation with a licensed mental health or medical professional, or legal professional, if needed.

First Printing: 2012

TABLE OF CONTENTS

Part One: Small Talk Starting Point

Initial assessment – challenges with interpersonal communication

Defining small talk and the big picture of communication Understanding your chit-chat goals & why you should talk to strangers

Finding your speaking voice

Part Two: Making the first move

Choosing the order of topics

Small talk helpers – starting phrases

Keeping the ball rolling: generating 'flow'

The Small Talk Recorder Sheet Exercise

Going deeper in the conversation

Part Three: Group Dynamics

Tips to use during the engagement of small talk in groups

Reading the non-verbal cues and clusters of a crowd

Part Four: Building Solid Rapport

The secret to speaking is active listening!

Using NLP (Neuro-Linguistic Programming) to gain rapport

Building rapport with effective non-verbal communication

Part Five: Meet the Public!

Outing to apply new techniques and achieve personal goals

Part Six: First Impression Management

Assessing where you are now

Some golden rules of first impression management

Using powerful 'social gifts' in daily interactions

The 7 fundamentals of a winning first impression

Body language and non-verbal communication for a positive vibe

Handshaking the right way

Managing non-verbal communication in the environment

Part Seven: Increasing your Charisma

Can charisma be taught?

How to develop charisma: twelve key moves

The art of storytelling

Creating your role-model

Part Eight: In Action – going forward in life

Network like a pro – key principle

The elevator pitch

Four networking articles

Reviewing online profiles for business or social connections

Additional References & Recommended Resources

Part One: Small Talk Starting Point

Initial Assessment:

You can't reach your destination of new goals without first understanding your current situation, and what's holding you back. It is important to not only hear feedback from your circle of influence, but to also self-assess your current strengths and weaknesses honestly. Please ask yourself these questions and record short notes:

1. What are my top 3 goals with interpersonal communication?
2. –What are my main strengths and weaknesses in interpersonal communications?
3. What are the main obstacles stopping me from achieving these new goals?
4. What opportunities do I have around me to help overcome these obstacles and/or achieve new goals of communication self-improvement?
5. On a scale of 1 to 10, ten being the highest, how willing and motivated am to actively change my habits to achieve new communication goals, as outlined in question one?

BONUS: to learn more about goal setting and why these above questions were chosen, you can watch the 2009 media interview with CBC News on my YouTube channel, called "How to Use GROW Coaching Model to Set

Goals." https://www.youtube.com/watch?v=S_CW3Zu0DLk

Defining Small Talk and the Big Picture of Communication

"Good communication is as stimulating as black coffee and just as hard to sleep ***after.***

"Anne Morrow Lindbergh – author and aviator

(1906 – 2001)

1. What do you think of this quirky quote? Does it ring true in your case?
2. Have you experienced this before, where you were so energized after a certain conversation that you couldn't sleep for a long time after? What caused it?
3. Why should you bother to "chit-chat"?

Small talk is more infamous than famous I think, because it can unnerve people quickly by either putting them in the proverbial 'hot seat' where they are being 'interviewed' with rapid-fire random questions, or it can unnerve people who feel they must generate interesting questions to ask without sounding or feeling FAKE. It's a challenge on both sides. So why do we do it and is it necessary?

Let me tell you a story (I like stories).

Several years ago, I was approached by a large government organization as they had a dilemma. They had an employee in a position of importance and authority who was very well educated, experienced and commanded technical expertise to absolutely do the required job, which was company auditing. The challenge was, before this individual could do the technical work of his job, he needed to start with an in-person meeting with the business teams of the companies he was working on to sort out the scope of the work and to get to know the people involved. Unfortunately, this government employee was lacking in interpersonal skills and essentially saw 'small talk' as a waste of time. His 'let's get right down to business' attitude made many people uncomfortable, unsure of an honest assessment, and they complained about him to his superiors. But what could the government organization do? He had excellent hard skills and produced the necessary correct results when he crunched the numbers. Could they fire him for not being friendly or shaking hands? To be honest – that was exactly what was on the table. That' s why they contacted me, because as a Communication Coach (in fact, the first Communication Coach in Canada!) they hoped I could guide this valuable senior manager in the way and the reasons to improve his interpersonal skills, for his own sake.

My first coaching session with him did not go well. Even I was put off by his apparent disregard for social norms, such as maintaining eye contact while shaking hands – two things he absolutely did not want to do. I assertively (perhaps too aggressively) instructed him on the value of first impression management and conforming to expected social graces of first meetings, and he was more than content to argue on an intellectual level that the small talk was a waste of time, and that he was being paid by the government to run serious business audits – not to make friends. We almost agreed to stop the coaching program right there. I couldn't quite understand how a man who had lived in two countries and who spoke three languages couldn't grasp these simple concepts of interpersonal behaviour.

Upon reflection, I decided to appeal to his PhD intellect, and the next session I brought him research and documents from other PhDs from the social sciences explaining their research on the importance of small group behaviour and rapport- building techniques, and he was intrigued. We then were able to finish our coaching program over the next few months and I am happy to report that he got quite good at smiling, shaking hands firmly and maintaining eye contact with me at the beginning and end of each of our sessions! He later received positive feedback from both peers and the manager that hired me, and his job was no longer in jeopardy. I can report that I grew as a Communication Coach with that one client, and I am grateful for that experience early on in my coaching career. Remember that story whenever you hear someone suggesting that small talk and interpersonal skills are not imperative in the business world.

Now, let's talk about the broader world of communication.

Defining Communication and the 3V effect:

My definition of "effective communication": You understand what I was trying to tell you. I understand what you were trying to tell me. No feelings were hurt during the process. I read your emotions correctly. This goes for any spoken, written or non-verbal communication. I applied good communication techniques in all 3Vs of communication, and the resulting 'vibe' was effective.

Questions:

Do you know what the 3V's of communication are, and why I named my company after them?

Have you ever heard of the so-called 7/38/55 'rule' in communications?

The company 3V Communications was founded in 2007 and is partly based on the work of Dr. Albert Mehrabian. One of his early but important studies showed that feelings and attitude were conveyed to others 7% through words, 38% by voice tone and 55% by facial expressions. Therefore 93% of this interactive communication was non-verbal!

But wait – this magic formula has been taken out of context over the years, by sociologists and interpersonal skills trainers just like me. The specifics of Dr. Mehrabian's studies are often overlooked. He was evaluating college girls only, small groups of about 20, looking at how their messages were received through words, voice and facial expressions, focusing on intended messages and feelings, and finally, a handful of his studies were combined to come up with the 7/38/55 "rule." When the studies were published in a popular magazine, the results were glossed over and generalized. That's how the public gained access to this easy formula.

However, all said, even though this was a limited study and cannot be applied too broadly to all communication interactions, it serves to remind us that the adage remains true:

"It's not what you say, but how you say it."

I have broadened the scope of the three original communication categories to create not just a tagline, but a philosophy of communication study: the 3Vs of communication.

Learn the 3Vs of Communication now:

VERBAL (our words, phrases, grammar, slang etc.)

VOCAL (our paralanguage: rhythm, speed, volume, intonation etc.)

VISUAL (body language & gestures, micro-expressions, attire, accessories, environment, etc.)

In a nutshell, to communicate our intended message most effectively, we need to have the 3Vs of communication working in alignment. This "3V effect" equals a 4th V – Vibe.

When there is synchronicity and harmony, the result is better confidence, better communication, and better rapport. This vibe is why we generally form an opinion about someone in just a few seconds as to their intelligence, style, friendliness, openness, trustworthiness, and so much more.

When any of the 3Vs are incongruent with the others it creates confusion and misunderstanding to your listeners. This miscommunication leads to lack of understanding and/or trust! Whether you are joining a group, managing staff,dealing with customers, making a presentation or speech, or managing your first impressions, you need to synchronize your 3V communications to align with your intended message and 'vibe'. That is the advantage of my 3V Communications holistic system.

Exercise: Applying the theory of 3V Communications Question: Using the 3V system, how would you show <u>confidence</u>?

Verbally I would...
Vocally I would...
Visually I would...

Your chit-chat goals:

Why should we bother to chit-chat? Because we can cut any tension and break the ice, we can open ourselves up for communication, and we can gain something, like a friend, a sale, a customer, a partner, etc.

Before you engage in small talk with anyone, anywhere, and at any time, you should ask yourself "What are my goals of this interaction/conversation?" Do I want to get a new business connection? Okay, but why? What is the real goal? It is to develop your network or your social/dating life. Please think of this larger goal for the interaction, not just the small goal of getting contact info/connected online. The big picture is to build rapport so that they like you on some level and trust you. The rest comes later once you have established a good 'vibe' and made a solid first impression.

Here's an article explaining well why we often don't talk to strangers, and why we actually should. Enjoy!

Why You Should Talk to Strangers

Research finds surprising benefits from connecting with new people. Published on November 19, 2014 by Art Markman, Ph.D. in Ulterior Motives Ulterior Motives

How goals, both seen and unseen, drive behavior by Art Markman, Ph.D.

I fly a lot. I have a typical routine on the plane. I pull out something to read or perhaps an iPad to watch a movie. I do my work. I don't generally engage in much conversation with the person sitting next to me, though sometimes I end up in a long conversation, and invariably, the conversation is great fun.

An interesting question is whether my travel would be more enjoyable if I engaged in more conversations with people I met on the plane? This issue was addressed in a fascinating paper by Nick Epley and Juliana Schroeder that appeared in the October, 2014 issue of the Journal of Experimental Psychology: General.

In two field experiments, they demonstrated that people generally avoid having conversations with strangers while commuting. One study queried train commuters: a second, bus commuters. During their commute, some participants were asked to imagine that they were told to have a conversation with another commuter they didn't already know. Those in a second group were asked to imagine that they were told to commute without talking to anyone. A third group got no instructions. Participants rated how much they thought they would enjoy their commute as well as how productive they thought they would be.

In this study, participants imagining they had to talk to another person thought they would enjoy the commute less than those who imagined sitting in silence. Those imagining they had to have a conversation also assumed they would be less productive on the trip than those who imagined sitting in silence. The control group came out in between on both measures.

A second set of field studies actually had commuters on the train and bus engage in conversations—or not. Members of a third group were given no instructions. Afterward, participants rated how much they enjoyed the commute as well as how productive they were. Participants also filled out a personality inventory.

Strikingly, participants who were asked to have a conversation with someone else on the train or bus really did have conversations. And these participants enjoyed their ride much more than those who had been instructed not to engage with other people, as well as those in the control condition (who also tended not to engage in conversations). Interestingly, participants in all conditions rated themselves as about equally productive.

If conversations like this are actually so enjoyable, why do people engage in them so rarely?

One other study asked commuters a variety of questions and

found that they underestimate how willing other people would be to talk to them. So commuters feel that they are much more interested having people choose to talk to them than other people are in being talked to. As a result, people avoid striking up conversations for fear of bothering another person.

Another study found that some people are able to predict their enjoyment of engaging in these random conversations. This study looked at people taking taxis leaving from an airport. Some participants were actually asked to engage in a conversation with the driver or to enjoy the solitude. As in the other studies, those who had a conversation with the driver enjoyed the ride more than those who did not.

In a second study, participants predicted their enjoyment. Those who routinely engage in conversations with the driver recognized that they enjoy the ride more when they talk than when they don't. People who rarely converse with the driver did not recognize that they would enjoy their ride more if they talked with the driver.

A final study examined another possibility: Perhaps the people who initiate conversations enjoy them, but those who do not initiate the conversations enjoy them less. That is, maybe the conversation is only positive for the initiator. This study was done in a psychology lab. Participants were waiting for the study to start. Some were instructed either to engage in a conversation with a second participant in the waiting room or to avoid having a conversation. Afterward, both participants were asked about how much they enjoyed the wait. Both the participant who initiated the conversation and the non-initiator enjoyed the wait more when they had a conversation.

Putting this all together, then, it seems like most of us are missing out on a big opportunity to enjoy our life just a little more. Many of us travel on trains, planes, buses, and taxis. In those settings, we generally elect to protect ourselves from interactions with other people. Yet, these data suggest that most of us would enjoy ourselves more if we had conversations with the strangers who sit near us rather than walling ourselves off.

These findings are particularly interesting, because technology makes it easier than ever to avoid connecting with strangers. Almost everywhere you go, people are engaged with smart phones and tablets. Because of those devices, we avoid connecting with the real live people sitting next to us—and it seems that we are missing out by doing so.

Source: https://www.psychologytoday.com/blog/ulterior-motives/201411/why- you-should-talk-strangers

Vocal Communication: Finding Your Speaking Voice

It is important to have a good speaking voice that is heard, non-threatening, calm, fun and memorable. Here are the key ingredients: rhythm, speed, volume and intonation.

Rhythm: This is the musical pace at which you deliver your 'lines'. 'Chop up' your sentences into chunks so that you are adding an imaginary comma or half-pause every 4-5 words. This will help create a rhythm that is easier to be listened to and followed. Think Barack Obama, for example.

Speed: Medium speed is the general rule, however there is something to be said for mirroring and matching other people's speed (and other voice qualities). Please remember that if you speak too quickly, it may sound like you are rushed and disorganized. If you speak too slowly, it may sound like you are unintelligent, or very tired and disconnected. If you do decide to mirror others at first, then make your plan to gradually bring the speed to medium for both of you.

Volume: Be loud enough to be heard and respected, but not the 'loudmouth' of the room! Being quiet is okay when actively listening, but not okay when actively speaking. We want others to hear us. Having said that, there is a technique that some people use where they purposefully speak quietly, thereby forcing others to lean in and really listen. It may work in some cases, but I am not a big fan of low- talkers or mumblers, so be cautious if using this technique. The reason why I urge caution is that the average person will not tell you when they don't hear/understand you, out of a sense of politeness. They will just nod and carry on! How will you know for sure?

Intonation: It is very important to add proper stress at the proper time. We need to pay attention to word stress (*i.e., what syllable in a word you emphasize*) and sentence stress (*i.e., which words you 'highlight' with your voice to indicate importance and add clarity to your sentence.)* Intonation is what I call the 'ocean effect' where your voice goes up and down in a nice rhythm, like rolling waves. We stress the content words (*nouns, verbs, numbers, etc*.) and those create the peaks of waves, and other non-essential functional words (*like articles, prepositions, conjunctions*) are de-stressed. When you combine this with appropriate rhythm, speed and volume, you create a great speaking voice!

If you think you need to work on your speaking voice, here are some exercises you can do by yourself or with a partner or coach:

Vocal Communication Exercises:

1. Breath control exercises

- Breathe calmly while waiting for your turn to speak. It helps control any nervousness
- Try the 'fake cigarette' exercise now where you pretend you are smoking
- Visualize cool, blue air in the nose, warm red air out the mouth
- Count to 4 while inhaling, hold for 4 seconds, and then exhale slowly for 8

2. Stress

- Syllable stress in a word: unBEARable, fanTAStic reSULTS
- Key word stress in a sentence: nouns, verbs, descriptors like adjectives, adverbs, numbers, universal statements and differentiators. For example:

"When you **hire** a **proFESSional web** desIgner, you **GUARantee** a **strong**, **comPELling** web presence in just **FIVE** days!"

"Using the **other** leading brand will **NEver** get you the **fanTAStic reSULTS** you're **GUARanteed** to get **EVery** time with **our** product."

3. Rhythm exercises

- Obey commas and see 'natural' pauses too, where a short pause would help
- Practice using difficult writing like Shakespeare
- Practice using rhythmic writing like poetry Shakespeare

"To be or not to be. That is the question"

"Like flies are to a wanton child, so too are we to the gods"

"How sharper than a serpent's tooth it is, to have a thankless child" "A horse! A horse! My kingdom for a horse!"

"Cry havoc and let slip the dogs of war!"

Poetry

Where do you think the pauses go? Try to read it different ways, playing with pauses.

Gifts – By James Thomson Give a man a horse he can ride Give a man a boat he can sail

And his rank and wealth his strength and health On sea nor shore shall fail.

Give a man a pipe he can smoke Give a man a book he can read

And his home is bright with a calm delight Though the room be poor indeed.

Give a man a girl he can love As I O my love love thee And his hand is great with the pulse of fate At home on land on sea.

4. Speed

- Say sentences really slow, then really fast, then find your 'normal' speed, with proper stress and rhythm
- Practice with tongue-twisters for added difficulty

If two witches were watching two watches, which witch was watching which watch?

How much wood could a wood-chuck chuck, if a wood-chuck could chuck wood?

Peter Piper picked a pack of pickled peppers. A pack of pickled peppers Peter Piper picked. But if Peter Piper picked a pack of pickled peppers, where's the pack of pickled peppers Peter Piper picked?

5. Volume

- Easy trick – speak to the person farthest away without yelling
- Practice speaking quietly, then loudly at home, to find the 'appropriate 'volume
- Make sure your feet are rooted, you are balanced and relaxed, and you resonate

6. Emotions

- Practice 'emoting' without words, using the ***Numbers vs. Letters exercise.*** This is where one person speaks to the other in an improv way only using random numbers to represent words. The other person in the role-play uses only letters as a language. You will notice how important a role body language and vocal communication play when a common language is not available – just like traveling to another foreign country!
- Be sincere for maximum results

- Once again, Shakespeare and poetry are ideal for practice, but anything will do!

This concludes Part One. Stay tuned for **Part Two: Making the First Move!**

Additional Notes:

Part Two: Making the First Move

"Don't knock the weather. If it didn't change once in a while, nine out of ten people couldn't start a conversation."

Kin Hubbard – cartoonist, humorist, and journalist

(1868 – 1930)

Write your answers down or discuss with a partner these questions:

Q1. Why do we talk so much about the weather?

Q2. How do you start a conversation with a stranger?

Q3. What happens when you can't think of anything to say? What should you do then?

Q4. Do you get nervous with someone new or someone in a higher status position? What can you do about those nerves?

Making the First Move with 3 Simple Steps

So, there you are at a party or function, and you want to make the first move, but you are scared. You are scared that they will not like you, that you will be rejected, that you will have nothing to say - the list goes on!

Guess what? They are probably thinking the same thing so don't worry about it!

Instead, take a deep breath, go over to the person and ask them an opening question. The active approach of introducing yourself gets more respect than the passive one of just waiting to be noticed. Think of yourself as being a 'host' rather than a 'guest', even if you are in fact not the host, and are a guest! It's in the mental attitude and proactivity. Big difference.

The fact that you are both there in the same room means that you have got something in common already. It's always best to start off with simple topics of conversation *(immediate environment, weather, food, etc.)* and then move on to what interests them. Remember to follow the simple formula of the three steps, or levels, of small talk.

First, we talk about the immediate environment, inside or out, which can be the weather, specific location etc. and internal environment i.e. the décor, the office set up, etc. Next, we talk about something safe and non-judgmental like facts, hobbies, reasons of activities of being there). Facts are not too debatable, and can lead to other topics of conversation, like last night's score of the hockey game, or the current affairs of what's happening in your city/country, etc. Finally, once you and your conversation partner are more comfortable with each other, you can move on to fun topics like ideas, opinions and values. We still need to be sensitive to how others may react to what we are saying though, but at least you are both warmed up and building rapport. As always, be careful with taboo subjects like sex, religion and politics.

This BONUS video from my YouTube channel called *"Let's Talk Small Talk and 3 Simple Steps to Build Rapport"*
will help explain this concept further.
https://www.youtube.com/watch?v=r6oGWWbZCAM

All the while, remember to "listen" with your eyes as well. Pay attention to their gestures, open or closed body language positions (*i.e., are their arms/legs open or crossed, are they leaning towards or away from you, etc.*), what is in their hands, etc. Be careful not to invade personal space. And remember:

"There are no uninteresting people, only disinterested listeners!"

The key is to let the other person do most of the talking, while you listen actively and continue to ask great questions. Be genuinely curious!

At the end of the conversation, they feel good and comfortable with you, and you have collected a lot of information to use for rapport building, plus perhaps you've done only a little talking yourself. This is a relief for shy and nervous people!

Here are some starter phrases and questions that you can use or modify to suit your preferences and unique situations.

Small Talk Helpers – Starting Phrases

Talking about the weather	• Beautiful day, isn't it? • Can you believe all this rain we've been having? • It looks like it's going to snow. • It sure would be nice to be on a beach right now. • I hear they're calling for thunderstorms all weekend. • We couldn't ask for a nicer day, could we? • How about this weather? • Did you order this sunshine?
Talking about current events	• Did you catch the news today? • Did you hear about that fire in Yorkville? • What do you think about this transit strike? • I read in the paper today that Yorkdale Mall is closing for renovations. • I heard on the radio today that they are finally going to start building the new subway line. • How about those Maple Leafs? Do you think they're going to win tonight?

At the office	• Looking forward to the weekend? • Have you worked here long? • So, are you working hard or hardly working? • I can't believe how busy/quiet we are today, can you? • Has it been a long week? • You look like you could use a cup of coffee. • What do you think of the new computers?
At a social event	• So, how do you know Justin? • Have you tried the cabbage rolls that Sandy made? • Are you enjoying yourself? • It looks like you could use another drink. • Pretty nice place, eh? • I love your dress. Can I ask where you got it?
Out for a walk	• How old is your baby? • What's your puppy's name? • The tulips are sure beautiful at this time of year, aren't they? • How do you like the new park? • Nice day to be outside, isn't it?
Waiting somewhere	• I didn't think it would be so busy today. • You look like you've got your hands full (with children or goods). • The bus must be running late today. • It looks like we're gonna be here a while, eh? • I'll have to remember not to come here on Fridays. • How long have you been waiting?

There are many ways to start a conversation, and many reasons why you should. Friendships can form, business relationships can sprout, and at the very least you can create a positive social interaction for someone and add a little sunshine to their life – if only for a moment. It is a good habit to get into – the habit of presenting yourself positively (i.e., open and friendly) to the world.

Keeping the Ball Rolling: Generating 'Flow'

Once you have got the conversation started you need to generate topics of conversation quickly, and with a good, comfortable sense of 'flow' that does not seem forced or randomly glued together. It needs to go from one topic to another seamlessly and without the appearance of effort. It cannot simulate an interview or a telemarketer's script.

KEY TAKEAWAY: At every opportunity, try your new small talk skills with clerks, sales staff, and bank tellers, and anyone that is paid to talk to you! Get good at it so it's there when you need it for dates, networking, interviews, client meetings and any other time you need to strike up a conversation or keep one going with a new colleague, friend or even a stranger. By practicing all the time, you are much more comfortable when the important meeting, interview or date comes around. Practice really helps a lot here.

HOMEWORK: Record a few of your new interactions, to train yourself to be 'in the moment' and listening with your eyes as well as your ears.

Starting Positive Small Talk: Conversation Record

Noticeable basic details of person	Environment and/or Situation	Basic details of conversation, remembered?
E.g. Kerri (*name tag*) Green eyes, blonde hair, Tattoo on her wrist	Grocery store clerk	Made her smile after previous customer made her frown. Talked about store's great cookies.

Going Deeper in the Conversation

Small talk is a great opener, but after that you need to keep the conversation going. If you can go deeper, it will not only extend the conversation, but it will enrich it.

Think of a conversation like a long rope with many knots spaced out. Each knot is a topic or 'hot spot'. When you come across one (or create one) the conversation can then go a new direction. Have some faith in the natural process of conversations by not trying to control the whole thing and steer every topic. Having said that, here is a great article on how to ask detailed, interesting and fun questions when you want to go deeper into the conversation or relationship.

10 Great Topics of Conversation by Peter Murphy

Don't panic. You can be interesting. Great topics of conversation needn't be difficult to think of. Think about this - what makes a topic interesting? Isn't it that people like to talk about it and that they have opinions on it? (Popular people use this to their advantage)

Once you realize that, you'll see that for interesting topics of conversation come from everyday life and things that we all have in common. Then you'll realize it's not so difficult to think of them.

Easy Solution to Great Conversation:

Don't think you have to be controversial and go for risky topics like politics and religion; you don't. In fact, to do so would be a mistake. Whatever topic you choose should make people relaxed and happy to talk; controversial subjects don't do that. Think instead about what all people share: families, hopes, dreams, experiences etc. Here are a few great topics of conversation to get you started:

1. Who is the most interesting person you ever met?

You can see how this would easily lead people to voice opinions and ask 'why?'

2. Where in the world would you most like to visit?

This dream location may be shared by others and so it makes people feel solidarity, but also, people will be itching to ask 'why?' and keep the conversation flowing.

3. ***What has been the most life-changing experience you've ever had?***

Here, people can share funny and touching stories if they want to, which will help you get a deeper understanding of them. Likewise, if people don't feel relaxed enough to give a heart-felt reply they can answer in a funny way and it all adds to the conversation.

4. ***What is the most spontaneous thing you've ever done?***

That opens the door to all sorts of funny and romantic stories.

5. ***Who's had the biggest influence on your life?***

Because this person has influenced the person you're asking, they must view them positively and have strong ideas about them. That means they're likely to enjoy talking about them.

6. ***What thing that you haven't yet done would you most like to do?***

This kind of inspirational question always gets people talking and everyone's usually happy to chip in with comments about people's hopes and wishes. Just be careful when commenting that you don't rain on their parade. It's their right to have whatever hopes they want.

7. ***What is the best quality you've inherited from either of your parents?***

This is particularly interesting at a family gathering when people know the parents you're talking about. It's also a bit of a bonding experience, speaking favorably about your parents.

8. ***From which person have you learned most in your life?***

This is another uplifting, positive topic of conversation that usually gets people talking.

9. What historical figure do you most identify with?

This lets you know something about the other people around you; it also opens up discussion of the events these historical figures were involved in. Yes, potentially it takes you into dangerous waters of politics and religion, but people usually take this question in the spirit of fun in which it's meant, so potentially awkward moments are easily averted.

10. What kind of music do you like?

You could then go on to talk of albums you've bought, songs downloaded or gigs you've been too. You might even ask - 'what's the most embarrassing album in your collection?' That's usually met with all-round hilarity!

These ideas should show you that interesting topics of conversation don't need to be complex or intellectual – in fact, the more ordinary the better, because then people feel qualified to talk about the topic.

Do remember: Neglect communication skills and you limit your happiness and success. And by default, you give others control over your life. The only way to be the master of your destiny is to take charge. Know what you really want and have the courage to stand up and be counted.

Suggestion: Watch this controversial TEDx talk called "How to Skip the Small Talk and Connect With Anyone" by Kalina Silverman. Read some comments. What do you think about it? Make notes on how you would feel if Kalina came up to you and asked you direct, probing questions. Then ask yourself how you would feel if a giant man came up and asked the same questions!

https://www.youtube.com/watch?v=WDbxqM4Oy1Y

This concludes Part Two. Stay tuned for

Part Three: Group Dynamics!

Part Three: Group Dynamics

We have all been invited to group gatherings of some kind, like family or class reunions, networking or professional development events, social parties at the office or at the corner pub. The common challenges that might cross your mind are:

1. How do I effectively 'read' the group?
2. How do I approach a group if I want to join their conversation/table?
3. How do I balance multiple conversations with many people and agendas?

To start, I would like to offer a fun way to bridge the previous two sessions with this one. You may recall back in the late 80's and 90's there was a TV series called **Star Trek: The Next Generation** *(TNG to us Trekkies!).* In that series there was a character named Data. He was an android who, like *Pinocchio*, aspired to become as human as possible. There are many interesting and funny scenes with him trying to learn and then adapt what he sees as proper human behaviour, and one of those adaptations came in the form of making small talk. I would like you to watch this short *YouTube* video (*if the link is still active – otherwise try to do a word search for the topic*) to start this chapter off. Video – Data writes a special subroutine for small talk

https://www.youtube.com/watch?v=9FqFm_vmVnE

This clip is from the episode entitled "Starship Mine." Briefly speaking, Data imitates a man named Commander 'Hutch' Hutchinsen who runs around the social gathering briefly chatting with everyone, asking interesting questions and making small talk. The problem is that his small talk is hurried and does not come off genuine at all. It sounds like a routine with no soul. In fact, most of the guests are annoyed by his small talk – not impressed. In the episode Data unfortunately imitates Hutch too well and comes off just as fake and forced in his attempts to shmooze the group. It is an interesting view of the wrong way to have effective small talk.

Now back to your challenges when approaching and entering a group setting. In a nutshell, you want to do this:

Observe

Sense the tone Enter with interest Leave with grace

To begin you need to slow yourself down before and as you enter the room. Before you go in, I want you to stop for a minute, breathe deeply a couple times (in through your nose, out through your mouth) and then walk in with eyes wide open (not literally). When you approach your designated group area or your chosen group to join, walk at a medium pace, with good posture, breathing well and with a 2% - 5% smile on your face. As you approach the group start observing their non-verbal communication including body language, hand gestures, feet positions and anything else that catches your eye. Let's break down some of the common non-verbal cues to look for.

Three Key Body Language and Non-Verbal Communication Concepts

1 – **Open vs. Closed**: Generally speaking, a person who is 'open' to conversation displays 'open' body language. This would most likely be the person's whole body is square to you, their arms are not crossed, their face is displaying calm/happy facial reactions to your approach *(i.e., not frowning, rolling their eyes, avoiding eye contact or wrinkling their nose!)* and they will even gesture to an open space, like a chair.

2 – **Toward vs. Away**: We humans are not too complicated on a non-verbal level. We display what we truly think and feel. It's up to the observer to catch it and interpret it correctly, and that can be a little tricky. Another general principle to look for is toward vs. away. We move towards people, things, ideas etc. we like and that will benefit us, and we move way from people, things, ideas that we don't like, or that threaten us in some way. As you move toward a person or group, observe if they 'retreat' in any way or if they lean or step toward you. That would be a good sign (*for*

example, someone stepping forward and extending their hand.) As you are chatting with people you can see their reactions to different topics of conversation in the same way. We all lean in and open our gestures to topics of interest, and retreat in some way on topics of dis-interest. The movements might be grand display gestures or just micro-expressions of the face that are hard to catch, but we all show what we are thinking and feeling. For more on this you may research Dr. Paul Ekman's work on universal micro-expressions of the face. You can find out more about this and even complete online training in this science of reading micro- expressions by visiting the Paul Ekman Group website http://www.paulekman.com/.

3. **Cues vs. Clusters**: When reading body language, please keep in mind that a single gesture is a cue, and by itself is hardly evidence of a person's thoughts and feelings. However, if we have 2-4 cues all indicating the same attitude or feeling, then this 'cluster' is more reliable. Always look for support before jumping to conclusions. Body language is an interesting science, but it is certainly not a 100% foolproof method of reading minds! If it were, our court systems would work very differently these days, correct? ☺

Here are some cues and clusters to practice and to look for:

IF YOU WANT TO DISPLAY…

Confidence:

Walk medium speed

Smile often when appropriate, showing teeth

Do not cross your arms or legs while sitting or standing.

At times rest hands on hips briefly

No fidgeting

No touching face, nose, head/hair Erect posture

Squared shoulders

Frequent eye contact with everyone

Trust & Reassurance:

Use large, open hand gestures in front of your mid-section

Hand to chest gestures or self-pointing with open hand (note: this does not include the common gesture women use when shocked or upset, as they touch their upper chest)

Nodding often where applicable

Symmetrical hand gestures that flow

Use open palm gestures

HOW TO READ WHAT YOUR GROUP IS FEELING…

Interested & Listening, Evaluating:

Sitting toward edge of chair

Body leaning forward

Wide-eyed

Head tilted 45 degrees, exposing ear

Tilted head supported by one hand

Hand on cheek, elbow on table

Stroking chin

Earpiece of frame of eyeglasses (or pen) in corner of mouth

Openness & Receptiveness:

Open hand and palm gestures

Unbuttoned coat/jacket

Exposed neck and mid-section

Moving up in their chair

Mirroring and matching your gestures

Smiling and nodding often

Good eye contact

Hands rubbing to show excitement

Legs not crossed (skirt wearing excepted!)

Bored or Indifferent:

Crossed legs, moving foot in a slight kicking motion Hips, bodies pointed or twisted away from you Head erect, not tilted

Backs straightens, then slouches

Glancing at watch, ceiling, phone, clock, other people, etc. Feet, hips, bodies pointed toward exit

Drumming on the table Tapping with feet

Pen clicking or finger tapping Doodling

Head in the palm of hand, eyes downcast Droopy or glazed over eyes

Blank stare with minimal blinking

Closed & Defensive:

Arms crossed on chest while listening/speaking

Making fists with hands reinforcing above defensive position

Arm-gripping, bicep-gripping

Sideways glances

Pursed lips, fake smile

Hand covering mouth

Feeling Superior:

Feet up

Sitting with the chair back serving as a shield

Peering over glasses that are halfway down bridge of nose

Arms spread out and gripping table (edges)

Leaning back, both hands clasped behind head, sometimes legs crossed

Steepling of hands

Hands joined together at back, chin thrust upward

Pointing at others or you

There are many body language cues and clusters. These are a few to get you thinking about your self-presentation, and to quiet your mind as you approach a group and see what pops in your head about their non-verbal communication. In truth the previous larger concepts about body language dealing with Open vs. Closed and Toward vs. Away will be much more beneficial to you as they are easier to see, compared to trying to pick up single cues and micro-expressions. At least you will now be more prepared to approach with calm confidence and have a solid guide on reading their feelings and attitudes toward you, and each other.

Exercise: How do you read these people? What are they feeling? Make some notes!

Social Party 1

Social Party 2

NOTES:

(Reference: The above 2 group depictions are from the book "How to Read a Person Like a Book" by Nierenberg and Calero).

Here are some quick phrase formulas you can use or modify as you see fit.

Strategies to Enter Group

Direct:

"Excuse me, can/may I join you/your group?"

"Sorry I couldn't help but overhear you discussing XYZ - could I join in/hear more/add an opinion on that?"

"Excuse me - sounds like a great conversation - could I join in?"
"Hi! This group looks fun! Mind if I join?"

NOTE: use open, confident body language too!

Exit Strategies

Hand off / introduce to other

"You should talk to Kate about this. She's the expert. Kate?"

"Well guys, I'm going to leave you three to figure out the world economy. I'm going to run now. Good luck!"

Summarize: thank them, action 1 (next steps), action 2 (just you-immediate), shake hands/leave.

"Well, thanks Bob. It's been great chatting with you. I'd like to connect on LinkedIn if you don't mind. I've got to run now and catch a couple people before they leave. Bye for now!"

This brings us to the conclusion of Part Three. Next time is

Part Four: Building Solid Rapport!

Part Four: Building Solid Rapport

"Listening, not imitation, may be the sincerest form of flattery." **Dr. Joyce Brothers**

"There are people who, instead of listening to what is being said to them, are already listening to what they are going to say themselves." **Albert Guinon**

Q1. What is a bad listener?

Q2. How can you tell if someone is really listening to you?

Q3. How can you build rapport with just verbal communication?

Q4. How can you build it with nonverbal communication?

Be a Great Listener! Use Active Listening Skills – Top 5 Tips

1. When you become an expert listener it means you are really paying attention and trying to understand not just the words being said but also the emotions behind them. You are listening TO words and FOR meaning!
2. When you go into an important meeting or other situation with someone, go into that encounter with only one thing on your mind - THEM. Focus and avoid distractions.
3. Use SOLER - This is a technique used by coaches, care workers and active listeners. It helps clients, co-workers or friends open up by leading by example. SOLER is:

S – Square yourself to the person and give them your full attention

O – Open posture, open arms (*uncrossed*) and uncrossed ankles too

L – **Lean** slightly towards the person, without invading personal space

E – **Eye contact** should be maintained 70-80% of the time, especially on important points of communication

R – **Relax** your body, shoulders, facial muscles, and voice to lead by example and encourage others to follow suit

1. Using **E.A.R.** will improve your active listening skills. Here is the explanation:

E – **Empathy** is a showing of a shared feeling and understanding of the emotional impact of the speaker's situation. Do not judge here, and please hold your own opinion. This is not the time to take over the conversation. Your job is to listen actively and pay attention to their emotional state and body language. Listen TO the words and FOR the feeling/meaning. This is why you must be making eye contact to be a good listener.

Also, listen intently for their real message, their core values, commitments, etc. by the specific language they are using. It's like seeing an iceberg in the water – we can't see the whole thing, but we know it is much bigger than the tip. The same is true for developing listening skills. Don't just listen to the surface words the person says. Listen for the underlying message, which is often emotional.

A - Acknowledge their wants, their pain. People want to be heard and understood, not necessarily always agreed with. When you say something like *"I hear you", "That would bother me too" or "I can understand why you're upset"* you are acknowledging their feelings, their point of view. You are not automatically agreeing or apologizing or anything like that. You are using empathy to acknowledge their truth.

R – **Relieve** pain and provide help if possible. Don't blame the person or pass the buck (responsibility) to another person on your team. Do your best to offer a solution or partial solution, or some way to relieve their stress. It doesn't always come down to a financial solution. Some things are more important than a refund or a voucher.

2. Please remember to be careful with starting your questions with *Why.* It usually sounds like you are challenging or criticizing the person, and in turn that person will get their back up and be on the defensive. It is not uncommon for short, 'snarky' or sarcastic responses to follow a perceived attack. To avoid this misunderstanding, try to avoid the word 'why' and of course, watch your vocal tone as well. For example, *"Why are you taking vacation now?"* could be changed to *"What are the reasons for requesting your vacation now?"* and *"Why didn't you wear a tie today?"* could be changed to *"I noticed you didn't wear a tie today. What was the reason you changed the company dress code today?"*

Exercise: Let's try to actively listen, paraphrase, empathize with a person, hear the true message, show you genuinely care, and get more details. Use EAR. Have an intellectual conversation with someone while actively listening for any emotionally charged words/topics that you can acknowledge.

PRACTICE TOPIC: "Your favourite food in the world is…because…"

Introduction to N.L.P. (Neuro-Linguistic Programming)

VAK Modalities in Use – Our 3 Languages

It is time now to learn a little about NLP – neuro-linguistic programming, and how we can often recognize the thinking process of a person by listening to the verbal indicators (words and phrases) that they use in everyday speech and then using this information to tailor the way that we communicate to them. We do this by reflecting to the person the same or similar words and phrases, and therefore build rapport by sending the message that we 'speak the same language'. This is good because it engenders trust and comfort, i.e., builds rapport. Why?

Because people like people, who are like themselves, or like who they aspire to be!

(This is a Tony Robbins quote.)

For example, if we meet someone who makes decisions because “It looks right” and uses mainly visual indicators, we will find it easier to communicate with and explain things to that person if we show him a diagram or ‘paint him a picture’ in his mind and use visual words and phrases back to him. He will immediately feel comfortable and sense that we are ‘on the same page.’ If communication is easy and comfortable, then he will most likely be open and receptive. This is good when we are trying to make a winning first impression and when we are managing partners and staff. It’s always a good habit to listen carefully to others and pick up on their favorite expressions and reflect to them the same words or notions. This is something you can try with friends, family and spouses. And the cool thing about this technique is you can use it with regular words and expressions too. It won’t be as effective as picking up a person’s VAK preference, but the principle is the same – reflect sameness.

The following is a list of words that indicate a *preference* for the **3** main modalities (**Visual, Auditory, Kinesthetic**) by the people using them. Which are yours?

Visual	Auditory	Kinesthetic	Neutral/Non-Sensory Based
Appear	Ask	Catch	Arrange
Bright	Be heard	Cold	Change
Dark	Call	Concrete	Consider
Dawn	Clear	Contact	Decide
Envision	Click	Feel	Distinct
Focused	Deaf	Grasp	Experience
Foggy	Discuss	Handle	Explain
Hazy	Dissonance	Hard	Get
Illuminate	Harmony	Heavy	Insensitive
Imagine	Hear	Hold	Know
Insight	Hearsay	Move	Learn
Look	Listen	Pressure	Motivate
Notice	Loud	Push	Notice
Perspective	Melody	Rough	Perceive
Picture	Quiet	Scrape	Process
Reflect	Remark	Slip	Recognize
Reveal	Resonate	Smooth	Remembering
Scene	Rhythm	Solid	Sense
See	Ring	Tackle	Think
Shine	Say	Tap	Understand
Show	Silence	Thrust	
View	Tell	Touch	
Vision	Tune	Unfeeling	
Visualize	Unheard of	Warm	
Vivid	Wave-length	Weight	

Below is a list of indicator phrases that people use. Which words and phrases do you use most often? Highlight them now.

Visual	Auditory	Kinesthetic
A blind spot	Afterthought	All washed up
An eyeful	Blabbermouth	Boils down to
Appears to me	Call on	Calm, cool, collected
Beyond a shadow of a doubt	Clear as a bell	Chip off the old block
Bird's eye view	Clearly expressed	Cool customer
Catch a glimpse of	Describe in detail	Come to grips with
Clear out	An earful	Control yourself
Dim view	Enquire into	Feel it in my bones

Eye to eye	Give me your ear	Firm foundations
Get a perspective on	Give you a call	Get a hold of/handle on
Get a scope on	Given amount of	Get a load of this
Hazy idea/notion	Grant an audience	Get in touch with
I see what you mean	Heard voices	Get the drift of it
In a flash	Hidden message	Get your back up
In hindsight	Hold your tongue	Grasp the idea
In light of	Ideal talk	Hand in hand
In person	Keynote speaker	Hang in there
In view of	Loud and clear	Heated argument
Looking closely	In a manner of speaking	Hold on (a second)
Looks like	Pay attention to	Hot head
Make a scene	Power of speech	I can't put my finger on it
Mental image/picture	State your purpose	Keep your shirt on
Mind's eye	To tell the truth	Lay cards on the table
Paint a picture	Tongue-tied	Pain in the neck
See to it	Tuned in/tuned out	Pull some strings
Shed some light	Unheard of	Scratch the surface
Short-sighted	Utterly	Sharp as a tack

Show me	Voiced an opinion	Slipped my mind
Showing off	Well informed	Slipped through my fingers
Sight for sore eyes	Within hearing	Smooth operator
Staring off into space	Word for word	So-so
Take a peak	Turn a deaf ear	Start from scratch
The naked eye	Rings a bell	Stiff upper lip
Tunnel vision	The same wavelength	Stuffed shirt
Under your nose	Makes him/her tick	Thick-skinned
Up front	Sounds like	Too much hassle
Well defined	Making music	Topsy-turvy
You'll look back on this	I'm all ears	Turn me on
	Music to my ears	Warm-hearted

Once you highlight the often-used words and phrases from the list, count the total in each category. Do you prefer to use visual, auditory or kinesthetic modalities? Knowing yourself is good and you can help guide people around you to better communicate ideas to you. This is a two-way street. Next assignment is to pay attention at work and try to start mapping people's communication VAK preference, and then using it with them.

Building Rapport with Effective Body Language

This is a great time to introduce the concept of 'mirroring and matching.' Mirroring is when we end up looking like a mirror image of each other while in conversation.

(Reference: from How to Read a Person Like a Book by Nierenberg and Calero)

Matching is when we end up doing the same gesture, posture or expression as the other person or people in the small group.

First, we need to understand that mirroring and matching happen naturally in everyday conversations that have good rapport. What NLP does, and what I'm suggesting you do, is speed up the process of getting to a state of great rapport, by consciously imitating what would happen naturally. This can be a very useful technique especially when time is limited, like an interview, a date, a networking event, a meeting etc. and you want to increase the odds of someone liking you, or at least feeling good while in your presence.

To build rapport quickly with people, we can consciously mirror or match their body language. We should not 'ape' all their body language exactly because of course they will notice that and ask us if we have gone crazy! We can do things subtle and covertly, and we do not need to imitate the body language 100%. We reflect the main idea, the main feeling. (This is the same idea as the previous concept, except now we are looking at and using body parts instead of words and phrases.)

For example, if you scratch your head, I might touch my cheek or temple, on the same side. If you lean forward in your chair, I might wait 3 seconds, and then slowly lean in too. Some small gestures I might imitate exactly, but most of the gestures I do will be a similar enough gesture that your sub-conscious reads it, but your conscious does not. I would also like to point out that you have a choice of what you are going to reflect to the person, and I recommend you mainly pick positive gestures, not negative or aggressive ones, for example.

BONUS Video on Ric's YouTube channel: "Mirror and Matching: The Magic of Rapport with NLP"

https://www.youtube.com/watch?v=5lxbtKfahrE

Tony Robbins has been around for many years as a life/career/motivational coach and speaker. Here is a video of him explaining and demonstrating the "magic of rapport" – please make notes or discuss this with your coach/partner.

VIDEO: Tony Robbins on how to build rapport, including mirroring and matching - https://www.youtube.com/watch?v=-9uHBEGpJm4

This chart below puts it all together – the different ways to build rapport with others, especially when you first meet them. You may use one, some or all these techniques at the same time, but that may produce 'cognitive overload' for you, so perhaps just a couple is enough until you get more practiced. Remember you are not being 'fake.' You are using communication techniques to speed up what would happen naturally, the building of rapport between strangers.

Building Rapport Quickly – On All Levels: How to increase levels of rapport

Match VAK Sensory Modalities/phrases ⇩

Match the person's physiology ⇩

Match their voice/energy ⇩

Match their breathing patterns ⇩

Match how they deal with information

Chunk Size ⇩

⇩

Match common experiences

EQUALS MEGA RAPPORT LEVELS!!!!!!!!

You can test your new skills all out in the next exercises, and then in your daily life for 'homework'.

Exercises: Paying Attention and Playing Imitation

In these exercises, we let the speaker (*your partner*) first talk for ***30 seconds or more***, while we 'calibrate' them and observe what we are looking/listening for (*according to the numbered exercises*). THEN we start to converse and reflect at them. Don't overdo it or it's too obvious and looks silly. ☺

1. Match the person's *visual, auditory and kinesthetic modalities*. Listen and reflect the other person's own favourite or preferred VAK words and phrases.

TOPIC: The benefits of eating fruits and vegetables daily.

2. "Mirror, Mirror, on the wall, who's the subtlest of them all?"

Catch their vibe, reflect it back, ride the wave together! Imitate same or similar body language, but not exactly. Watch especially eye and hand movement, leaning, smiling, etc.

TOPIC: The importance of gym class in all years at all levels of education!

3. *Voice-over!* Here is your chance to act! Imitate the rhythm, speed, volume and intonation of their voice. Can you match their breathing patterns as well? Also try to use their favourite words and interjections, including umms, ahhs, wells, yeahs, etc.

TOPIC: The relationship between Canada, the US and the UN.

4. Put it all together and find commonalities. Find a link between you and your partner. Anything will do!

TOPIC: How did you get here today?

Practice as much as you can and get ready for your next adventure in **Part Five: Meet the Public!**

Part Five: Meet the Public!

Wherever I go meeting the public... spreading a message of human values, spreading a message of harmony, is the most important thing.

Dalai Lama

QuoteAddicts

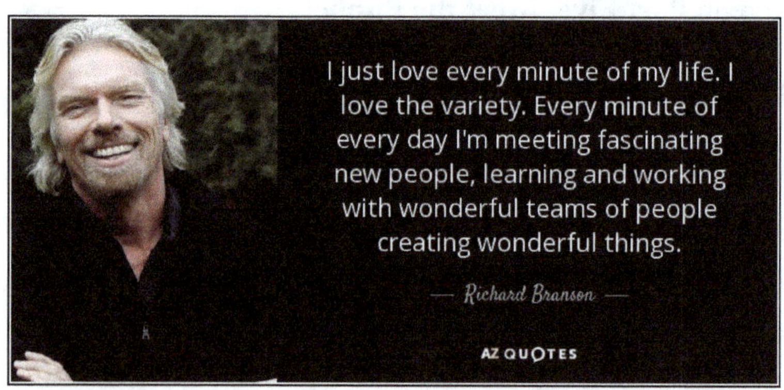

It's time to put your small talk skills, both verbal and non-verbal, to the test. Review your notes, videos, formulas and exercises so far, and get ready to apply them in public.

Go out to a large mall or plaza, walk around and pop into stores randomly. Inquire about their product or service but remember to make interesting small talk first, and don't take up too much of their time if you're not going to buy anything. Service industry folks are often very good naturally or receive training in interpersonal communication, like small talk and moving a conversation forward, so you can not only practice your skills but maybe learn a few things along the way! If you have a partner-in-training or a coach, take them with you. Give it a go! Try at least 4 shops/stores. Stretch your comfort zone

After the public outing, move on to **Part Six:**

First Impression Management!

Part Six: First Impression Management

Making a Winning First Impression

"You never get a second chance to make a first impression."
Anonymous

*"I usually make up my mind about a man in ten seconds, and I very rarely change **it.**"*

Margaret Thatcher (1925 – 2013) Fmr U.K. Prime Minister
Quick assessment:

1. What are some positive characteristics of your typical 1st impression? List at least 3.

1

2

3

2. What are some negative characteristics of your typical 1st impression that you would like to improve? List at least 3.

1

2

3

3. Does your typical 1st impression differ between work and social functions? How/Why?

Some Golden Rules of First Impression Management

(Based on "First Impressions: What You Don't Know About How Others See You" by Ann Demarais, Ph.D & Valerie White, Ph.D.)

The Primacy Effect – The first information you see or learn about someone is weighted more heavily than what you learn later.

The Halo and Horns Effect – If we meet you for the first time and you seem upbeat; we assume you are also smart, likable, and successful. If you complain a lot or otherwise start off with a negative attitude, we assume you are also boring, unsociable, and weak.

How do we make others feel good in a business or social situation? We need to be 'socially generous' and try to satisfy (*in a balanced way*) the things people seek out from their social interactions, which are the **4 Social Gifts:**

Appreciation – show understanding, empathy, sympathy, acceptance, respect for his/her talents, qualities etc.

Connection – find where you intersect. Identify similarities and give a sense of being understood and a sense of belonging. People like people who are like themselves.

Elevation – people want to be in good spirits, laugh, uplifted. So, smile, be playful, entertaining, and positive.

Enlightenment – we all like to learn something new. Share something that makes you stimulating and appealing, without going off like a boring professor at a lecture! ☺

(NOTE: In some of my coaching and training, and in my 2016 TEDx talk, I have combined the ideas of the last two social gifts to become one: **Positivity**.)

SUMMARY: You can make others feel good after interacting with you if you *appreciate* them for who they are, *connect* to them, *elevate* their mood, and stimulate them with new ideas and perspectives through *enlightenment*.

1. **Ways to Focus:**

   1 – How you feel about yourself

   2 – How you feel about the other person

   3 – How the other person feels about you

   4 – How the other person feels about him/herself

You can affect how others feel about you, and about themselves. How people feel about themselves after interacting with you will impact how they feel about you as a person.

Using the Magic of Social Gifts in Daily Interactions

Appreciation

I appreciate your interest in keeping costs down while doing business with our company.

I appreciate you taking time out of your busy schedule to meet me.

I appreciate a person who has great taste in art!

I can appreciate that you have English as a second language, and that this task must not have been easy for you to complete. Well done!

I admire a person who can fix a computer in minutes. I can see you really have a talent for negotiations.

Connection

Let's (re-)connect over lunch, okay?

Thank you for connecting with me regarding this issue.

We technical folks need to improve our soft skills as well, eh?

We all want to go home early, but we also all have responsibilities here to complete.

We need to find a win-win here that will benefit us both.

Agreed?

Elevation

Wow what a wonderful day today eh?

This sunshine is making me smile all day today!

Hey, that's a great bag/phone/car/etc. Is it new?

Let me tell you a funny story: a horse walks into a bar. The bartender asks,

"why the long face?"

John, I really appreciate you working late last night. It really helped me out a lot. Thank you so much.

Enlightenment

Did you know that... Statistics say that...

I read in the paper today that... I read online that ...

Back in my home country/town, we do/eat/say/act ...

I am reading a book about XYZ. It is really fascinating. It says that... Have you ever noticed...?

Assignment: Place a yellow stickie note near your desk/phone/desktop for a week, so it reminds you every time as you are responding to calls and emails to add Appreciation, Connection, Elevation and/or Enlightenment (or Positivity) to your dialogues.

The 7 Fundamentals of a First Impression

(Based on "First Impressions: What You Don't Know About How Others See You" by Ann Demarais, Ph.D & Valerie White, Ph.D.)

Accessibility – Your openness. There are 2 key components – your style of making contact (whether you take the initiative to introduce yourself, what mood you project, how actively you set a comfortable tone) and the content (what you actually say.)

Showing Interest – Ask open-ended questions and use active listening.

Subject Matter – Follow the 3Fs: **Field** (comments on present location, inside or out), **Facts** (what's happening in the local news/world/company), **Fun** (ideas and opinions about anything that comes up, as long as both parties are comfortable.) It's still a good idea to avoid topics on sex, religion, politics etc. to be safe.

Self-Disclosure – sharing personal information, your experiences, feelings, dreams, challenges. Discussing objective topics is your intellectual self-presentation and self-disclosure is your emotional self-presentation. Revealing yourself makes you more interesting, likable, and makes others more comfortable with you. It also allows you to control the pace at which you develop the relationship, fast or slow.

Conversational Dynamics – Energy and connection. It's the feeling, the vibe associated with the conversation, independent of what is being said. There are 2 parts: the Energy that you put out – how much you talk, how fast, how loud, and Synchronicity – how you take turns, yield or hold the floor, find a mutually satisfying rhythm. A good conversation will go back and forth between parties.

World Perspective – How you see yourself and the world you live in. Are you viewed as relaxed or an alarmist? In control or a victim? Flexible or rigid? Do you project a sense of superiority or inferiority? Are you positive or negative?

Subtle Sex Appeal – More than sexuality, more than flaunting your body or showing skin. Sex appeal is a sign of your openness and engagement. The process is the way you show your appeal – through your appreciation for and attraction to others and with your physical confidence. Your style is how aggressively, passively, or playfully you present your sexuality. Sexuality is about responsiveness, showing people that you find them attractive or interesting. This really has nothing to do with dating – it's about social flirting and self-presentation, regardless of the genders in the parties.

Homework: How do you rate yourself in the above 7

fundamental areas? Re- assess your first impressions and add/subtract what is needed to create a winning first impression – every time.

The Approach: If you want to make a confident first impression, whether it is at an interview or on a date (same thing, right?), giving a speech or selling a product, do a 'head-to-toe' pre-check before you enter the room and/or start talking.

Body Language and NVC for a Positive Vibe: (From Handshakes to Head Nods!)

Here is a "head-to-toe" pre-check that you can do before important meetings:

Head:

Are your facial muscles relaxed and not tense? Are you smiling?

Are you showing teeth naturally when you smile?

Are you nodding often to show agreement and encourage connection? Are you making plenty of eye contact?

Voice:

Are you loud enough to be heard and respected?

Are you adjusting to the volume of the group or situation? Are you controlling your pace evenly?

Are you using pauses for dramatic effect correctly? Are you stressing your key words and phrases?

Body:

Are your shoulders relaxed?

Is your back straight, including your neck? Is your chest tilted up slightly?

Are your arms loose, not tightly squeezed into your body?

Are you leaning towards the person, without invading

personal space?

Are your arms uncrossed, regardless of the temperature?

Arms & Hands:

Do your gestures match and/or accentuate your stressed words and phrases? Are they moving at an appropriate speed, avoiding jerky movements?

Are they avoiding wringing in nervousness?

Are they out of your pockets, off your lap mostly and not hidden under a table? Are they avoiding fidgeting with pens, phones or your hair?

Are the palms facing up and open?

Are you avoiding accidentally pointing with a finger?

Legs & Feet:

Are your legs uncrossed?

Are your legs slightly open, balanced?

Are your feet pointing towards the person and not the door? Are you avoiding tapping and bouncing your feet while sitting?

From now on, whether you are working, walking in the street, shopping, doing a presentation or meeting for work, on a social outing or date, etc. pay attention to the power of your body language and voice!

Bonus Video: One of the most watched TED Talks is Amy Cuddy's *"Your Body Language Shapes Who You Are."* If you haven't seen it, watch it now:

https://www.ted.com/talks/amy_cuddy_your_body_language_shapes_who_you_are

Handshakes:

Here is some advice when meeting new people or when in a more serious situation like an interview or business function. To start, 'medium' is the rule to remember. Walk at a medium pace, speak with medium voice/volume, gesture and shake hands with medium speed. This shows you are calm and in control of yourself.

After a calm approach, you should make sure you are engaged in eye contact and then smile as you extend your hand. Maintain good posture as you approach and extend the hand. Don't bend at the waist (unless in Asia or with Asian delegates) and don't over-extend your arm so you appear too eager and/or off-balance. Introduce yourself (e.g., Hello – I'm Ric. Nice to meet you!) and connect hands (not fingers) evenly, palm to palm. Be 'firm but fair' to the other people in your networking circles! Never crush a hand and never offer a seemingly 'broken wrist' or 'just-fingers' weak handshake. Both hands should be level – do not twist the hands to either extreme side, if possible. I am not a fan of twisting someone's hand so that my palm is up, and they have 'the upper hand' now, or vice versa. Let's start off on equal footing, shall we?

Pump your hands 2-4 times, gently and evenly, and repeat the person's name after they introduce themselves to help you retain that new information. There is usually no need for extra tactics, like using your free hand to clasp the hands while shaking (the double) or patting the shoulder of the person you are engaging (the pat-down). In the North American culture these extras are not necessary, but if someone does that to you, it's almost natural to return the favour, to even the score. Go ahead and do unto others as they do unto you.

Dominant people may want you to enter a room first and will gesture to let you go first, and may even lightly touch/pat your back, as a 'guide' through the doorway. It looks polite (and it technically is) but it also is another example of them 'steering' you somewhere and being in control because they can see you the whole time, and you need to 'trust' them when they're behind you. In evolutionary terms, you never wanted a potential predator or someone you didn't know/trust to be behind you where you're vulnerable to blind attack.

Regardless of what is in their mind or their style of greeting, you should always aim for a balanced and equal meet to start the relationship on the right foot. Just don't be surprised if others have favourite tactics they wish to use on you. It's all practice!

When President Donald Trump came onto the political scene (the first term) everyone was talking about or experiencing firsthand, his "Trumpshake". He would pull people into his centre line and off-balance them. The reason could've been out of habit, for power imbalance, or another reason, but it caused scenes and media conversations to be sure. Here is a blog article I wrote on the subject, as well as a short video by Macleans.

Blog Post/Video here:

http://www.communicationcoach.ca/blog/what-does-your-handshake-say-learn-these-tips/

Managing Non-Verbal Communication in the Environment*:*

What is non-verbal communication? One thing that frustrates me as a Communication Coach is when I hear media or even 'experts' state that non-verbal communication is body language. We have to understand that non-verbal communication is the biggest piece of the communication pie, and it consists of body language, yes, but it also consists of voice and para-language, and anything the eye can see like clothing, jewelry and other accessories, brands and labels, what kind of car, smart phone or tablet you have, and how you set up a (virtual) room or office. It is a huge piece of the communication pie, so do not ignore the other aspects mentioned in favour of focusing only on physical gestures.

Pay attention to your surroundings. Set up a room or table before a meeting to send the right message of openness and friendliness. Do not have things like lamps, tall pictures, menus, etc. in your way and especially blocking your line of sight. Do not build a 'Great Wall' on your desk at work that sends the message "Do Not Approach!"

When meeting someone at a café or restaurant try to get there first and pick the seating area that has less noise and distractions. Choosing a small two-person table will ensure they sit across from you, not beside you. Sit with your back facing the wall so that your conversation partner will not have distractions catching their eye, and they can focus on you. Note that about 90% of people (not including me □) are right-side dominant (i.e., right-handed) and are most comfortable when their dominant side is toward the other person. Use this if possible and try to line up your right eye to theirs when making eye contact.

Here are videos on body language for business. In 2014 I was asked by the global company Firmex to produce two videos for them about a) Body Language in the Boardroom, and b) Using Body Language to Close Deals. They can be found searching those titles, or here if you are reading the eBook.

https://www.youtube.com/watch?v=Gf4pxwwPgXg
https://www.youtube.com/watch?v=myRU0zrDqeQ

I hope you have enjoyed Part 6 and have picked up on a lot of tips and techniques to plan and then manage your many first impressions. I believe in the importance of understanding first impressions so much that when invited to speak at a local TEDx conference in 2016 I chose this very topic. My TEDx talk is “The Long Life of First Impressions” and can be found on the TEDx site, or on YouTube.

https://www.youtube.com/watch?v=SuG-BHquAHU

If you like it, please ‘like’ and share to your social networks. The importance of interpersonal skills in today’s tech-world cannot be underrated or undervalued. I appreciate your help in spreading the idea!

See you next time with **Part Seven: Increasing Your Charisma!**

Part Seven: Increasing Your Charisma

Starting Quotes:

"There is a long list of psychology research demonstrating that appearances matter more than most of us would care to admit. As shallow as it may be, better- looking people have been shown in various studies to have higher self-esteem and more charisma, are considered more trustworthy and are better negotiators."

Andrew Ross Sorkin (1977 -) American journalist and author

"Charm is an intangible. Chutzpah, charisma, that kind of thing, you can't buy it. You either have it or you don't."

Colm Feore (1958 -) American-Canadian stage, film and television actor

"My dad's a minister, meaning that he's full of charisma. If he's telling a story about Noah's ark, you best know each tiger is going to be having their own little conversation and narrative."

John Boyega (1992 -) English actor

"Being a leader gives you charisma. If you look and study the leaders who have succeeded, that's where charisma comes from, from the leading."

Seth Godin (1960 -) American author, entrepreneur, marketer, public speaker

(Want more? http://www.inc.com/kevin-daum/25-quotes-to-inspire-charisma.html)

Discussion

1. What is charisma and how much do you have (*in your opinion*) on a scale of 1-10?

2. Tell me about someone you know who has a lot of charisma. What makes them special? Please write a few adjectives down.
3. Are things like charisma and confidence abstract, emotional ideas that cannot be taught? Why or why not?
4. If you decided today that it would be a good idea to increase your charisma,how would you go about doing that? HINT: Think 3Vs…

Can Charisma Be Taught?

By Dr. Woody

The Career Hot Seat Published April 09, 2012 FOXBusiness

Read more: http://www.foxbusiness.com/personal-finance/2012/04/09/can- charisma-be-taught/

Great leaders are inspiring. They touch us in ways that make us believe in the cause--whether it's making quarterly sales numbers or taking to the streets in protest. We feel compelled to take action.

A person's ability to touch and motivate others is often referred to as charisma.

Throughout history, charisma has been viewed as a special trait or ability that just comes naturally to a select few. Essentially, it's the notion that "great people" are born and not made, an idea many still believe. Consider that when we describe charisma, it's usually in terms of the individual as opposed to the concept.

So, this begs the question: Can charisma be taught?

According to Olivia Fox Cabane, author of The Charisma Myth, the answer is yes. Cabane rejects the notion that charisma is purely driven by inborn traits and abilities, a notion most psychologists agree with. Human behaviors are driven by a more than just our natural attributes: Context, environment, and our ability to learn certainly play a role in developing behavior.

Cabane views charisma as a set of behaviors that she believes can be taught to anyone if they are willing to put in the time and effort. She explains that charisma is really about getting people to do what you want them to.

For the most part, Cabane's techniques to learn charisma are focused on changing your mindset to influence your body language. The idea is to provide individuals with the tools necessary for accessing, honing, and utilizing their assets to influence others to action. However, it's not just about simple tricks. Cabane notes that it's important to be genuine in how you project yourself because "we are terrible liars as human beings" and people will pick up on fake attitudes and disingenuous offers.

Learning charisma starts with reshaping your mental state and then manifesting those changes through physical gestures that accurately project that mental state.

Cabane defines charisma as being comprised of three elements: presence, power, and warmth. Cabane believes charismatic individuals possess varying degrees of each trait that combine to manifest as a form of personal magnetism. Here are the three traits:

Presence. Presence is being fully focused, aware, and engaged in what you are doing. Whether driving a car or having a conversation, you must be present in order to be as effective as possible. One of the greatest impediments to presence is our internal monologue. "It's hard to be fully present in an interaction when your brain is beating yourself up," she says.

We've all experienced self-criticism and how it can bring us down. Cabane advises her clients to use meditative techniques to clear their minds before engaging in interactions that will require them to demonstrate confidence and engagement.

Power. We have a tendency to evaluate others through our interpretations of their style and body language, and according to Cabane, people typically accept what you project.

It's critical to project the right image if you hope to influence those around you. The way you dress and act can have a tremendous impact on how others see you. Cabane recommends tweaking your physical state (dress, grooming…) so as to impact your own psychological state and boost confidence.

Warmth. Cabane says that projecting warmth is the toughest of the three charisma components to teach. "Warmth," she explains, "Simply put, is goodwill toward others."

However, the goodwill you intend may not always come across in your body language. To remedy this, you have to understand your message first and then match your body language to that message. Simple behaviors like the way you angle your head in conversation can make the difference between being perceived as arrogant or warm.

It's important to remember that we can't change our personality, but we can change our behavior. There are certainly traits that predispose some individuals to learning and demonstrating charismatic behaviors better than others. It's no different in the sports world. There are countless examples of athletes who were able to overcome perceived physical limitations only to break the standards for achieving success. The same can be said for learning charisma. It all starts with the mind. As Cabane explains "whatever your mind believes, your body will manifest."

Michael "Dr. Woody" Woodward, PhD is a CEC certified executive coach trained in organizational psychology. Dr. Woody is author of The YOU Plan: A 5- step Guide to Taking Charge of Your Career in the New Economy and is the founder of Human Capital Integrated (HCI), a firm focused on management and leadership development. Dr. Woody also sits on the advisory board of the Florida International University Center for Leadership.

Exercise: Analyze your Presence, Power and Warmth!

Charisma is All in the Ears

(By Patrick Kampert, Tribune staff reporter. Chicago Tribune. Chicago, Ill.: Aug 6, 2006.)

Barack Obama has it. Your cousin Ernie doesn't. Vince Vaughn has it. And maybe you wish you had it.

The "it" is charisma. Everyone has some. But if you don't naturally have buckets of it like Bill Clinton or Oprah Winfrey, can you develop more of what you have?

You betcha, says Howard Friedman, distinguished professor of psychology at the University of California at Riverside.

"Like any change in personality, charisma improvement takes time and practice," he said in an email.

Charisma isn't just based on physical features either, he said, adding that it has to do with "emotional communication and emotional expressiveness."

Jane Alderman, the dean of Chicago casting directors and who recently portrayed Vaughn's mom in "The Break-Up," says the Chicago- area native's charisma has little to do with being tall. "Vince is a very strong, kind person who's hysterically funny," she said. "But he's probably one of the best listeners I know. He makes everybody feel good; he makes them feel included."

Social scientists like Friedman are able to measure charisma by analyzing non- verbal communication and watching how observers react to certain individuals.

Tips to take you from blah to being somewhat brilliant:

“Charisma isn't something you can manufacture,” says Alderman. But psychologists say all of us can develop more of the "it factor" we already have. Here are some tips from local experts that can help you, whether you're a corner-office king or a cubicle dweller.

Be open about your passions. Chicago author and corporate trainer Rob Sullivan (careercraftsman.com) says that, on a scale of 1 to 10, most people express their emotions in a range of 4 1/2 to 5 1/2. Charismatic people, he said, tend to work above that range. "People have to be willing to share their passions. Most people are afraid to share who they are."

Listen with your eyes. Many people who attend the Second City Training Center have no illusions about a "Saturday Night Live" career, said Rob Chambers, president of training and education at the famed improv institution. Some want to improve their self- confidence; others want to meet people. Chambers and his staff help them learn to read a room, "picking up signals that people are giving, whether it's verbal, physical, emotional or psychological." Most of the information we get in a meeting, he said, is non- verbal.

Be other-centered. "Self-confidence does not mean self-involved," Chambers said. Ask questions of the people you're with, he said, and listen to them talk without jumping ahead in your mind and figuring out what you're going to say in response.

"If you're not listening and not observing," added Alderman, "you can't assess what other people's needs are."

Tell stories. Sullivan calls this creating your own "verbal movie trailer." He recently helped some young graduates improve their interviewing skills. One woman trying to get into nursing school simply said she wanted to help others. Sullivan pressed her, and it turned out she had spent weeks at the side of her boyfriend in the hospital. She saw how nurses made a huge impact in people's lives and later shadowed a cardiac neonatologist for a week, deciding to make that her specialty. Her story showed her strong character and charisma, Sullivan said.

Have a strong work ethic. "In films and television, just as in life, the people who get noticed are the ones who have done their homework and are prepared when they get their turn," Alderman said. "Don't take anything for granted or have a sense of entitlement," she added. "You have to be willing to understand that this has to do with being prepared."

How to Develop Charisma: Twelve Key Moves

By Debra A. Benton www.debrabenton.com

You've seen them. People like John Edwards or Carly Fiorina whose personal magnetism makes them stand out and propels them up the ladder of success.

But is charisma -- that powerful personal magic that attracts people and promotions like a magnet -- something you are born with or something you can learn?

It's common knowledge, for example, that the late president John F. Kennedy exuded charisma. Yet historians say his style was so carefully rehearsed that before running for president he even commissioned a study to determine the most effective handshake!

Those who study the phenomenon of charisma say while some people are innately more charismatic than others, there are certain things everyone can do to boost their charisma quotient. Debra Benton, author of **Executive Charisma: Six Steps to Mastering the Art of Leadership** offers the following pointers:

Expect acceptance.

Regardless of rank, expect to be treated as an equal. If you expect acceptance, you just might get it. If you don't expect it, you definitely won't get it.

Control your attitude.

Success in business is based more on mental attitude than on mental capabilities. Be optimistic toward yourself, others and life. Walk in to a room with a spring in your step and a smile on your face.

Perfect your posture.

Pull your ribcage away from your pelvis, roll your shoulders back and down, pull your stomach in and tuck your bottom toward your spine. Breathe deeply. You'll not only look better, but feel more energized, alert and in control.

Think before you talk.

Think fast, pause, then speak purposefully. One CEO practices saying everything to himself before he says it out loud so that he will hear how it sounds and can change it if he needs to.

Slow down.

Speed in speaking, moving, gesturing and walking looks nervous and scared. Scared people get passed over, not hired or promoted. Learn to speak in a comfortable, easygoing and welcoming way. Don't waste time, but do speak as if you have all the time in the world for those you are speaking to.

Shoot straight.

Everything you say or write can be done in a simple, straightforward manner.

Just do it.

Be a good storyteller.

People understand you better, remember what you say longer, and find you smarter and more interesting if you use anecdotes to make your points.

Be aware of your style.

Clothes don't make the man but they do make a difference. Wear well-tailored, good quality clothes that make you look like you are in charge. But remember, it isn't as much about your look as how you look at things and what people see when they look at you.

Admit your mistakes.

If you are error-free, you're likely effort-free.

Don't be bullied.

If you are unjustly criticized, don't take the bait and get into an argument. Instead calmly ask: "Why do you think that?" "What do you mean?" or "What's that based on?"

Be flexible.

Be able to stand out while still fitting in with the crowd.

Be at ease with yourself and others.

Look others straight in the eye, eliminate any defensiveness and take the edge off your voice. Never let them see you sweat!

Exercise: How do you match up with the above key components of charisma?

Give examples of your hits and misses.

BONUS VIDEO: 9 Mistakes That Kill Your Charisma:

https://www.youtube.com/watch?v=R20DrhsdJaQ&feature

Next write down the top 3 things you will immediately start to work on to increase your charisma:

1.

2.

3.

The Art of Storytelling

You will notice that 'story-telling' was often mentioned in the articles on charisma. Story telling is a key ingredient to not only being more charismatic, but also being more memorable and a better communicator of ideas all around. Make real effort to improve this area of your skill set to include both serious and humorous stories.

Are you perhaps wondering why "storytelling" is in here? Perhaps thinking it's childish, irrelevant or too simple? Take a look at what these folks think about it:

"Facts alone are not enough; you have to do storytelling."

Vinod Khosla (1955 -) Indian-American engineer, billionaire venture capitalist

"Storytelling is everything. Show me an MBA and your sales numbers, that's fine. But tell me a great story and how you got started and your vision, and we'll talk."

Barbara Corcoran (1949 -) American businesswoman, real estate mogul and investor, author, and judge on TV show "Shark Tank"

"Storytelling is the most underrated skill."

Ben Horowitz (1966 -) American businessman, author, partner of Andreessen-Horowitz venture capitalist investments

"Storytelling can be used to drive change."

Sir Richard Branson (1950 -) English business magnate, Founder of the Virgin Group, billionaire investor and philanthropist

If I asked you to tell me a couple good (i.e., funny) jokes, could you? I bet you could come up with at least a couple of your favourites on the spot. But where did they come from originally? Was it 'passed down' to you by your dad, your sister, your best friend? Do you remember the moment that you first heard that joke, even if it was many years ago? I do. And that's the power of storytelling. If we can recall the person, emotional impact of the moment and the joke itself and then re-tell it well, that's charisma in action, and that's how we humans have been carrying on for thousands of years! We tell stories to share knowledge, give warnings, create community and many other reasons.

Please take a moment to read this article and watch this illustrative video regarding story telling.

http://www.theglobeandmail.com/report-on-business/careers/career-advice/life-at-work/three-simple-strategies-for-keeping-your-edge-at-work/article28081974/
https://prezi.com/lvln-7xg-tr6/the-storytellers-secret/

You will notice the name Carmine Gallo mentioned in both resources. He is a fellow communications expert and has written great books on the secrets of storytelling and TED talks. I like his style, so I have referenced him a couple of times. If you like his style too you can seek out his books or his free newsletter on his website.

TASK: Prepare one or two GREAT jokes that involve telling more than a one- liner. Practice telling the story in an engaging way. Set the story up well so we know relevant background of place/character(s), what type of adventure/struggle they were on, and the moment of 'discovery' or climax i.e., the 'punch-line'. Deliver it well to get laughs but also to practice being a good storyteller.

Task Two: Tell a serious but fun story from one of your recent days off, vacation or holiday. Try enriching the event with details. For example, instead of just stating facts, like *"A while ago Sam and I went to Cuba for a week, and we had a good time"* slow down and give more details that are rich with imagination. For example:

"A year ago, Sam and I went to Cuba for a week. We had never been before but thought it would be like Mexico. How little prepared we were for the culture shock when we arrived! A moment after getting to our hotel, ... (this happened) and the next day ... (another event) ... and ... "

The devil is in the details. Paint a picture in people's minds. Let them imagine being there with you. Don't rush. Let them get interested/excited/curious about what happened next. Focus on the fun details that move the story along, not the small details that do not. I don't want you telling every little detail and then losing your audience because your story is too long! Balance between people/events and relevant detail is the key.

Creating Your Charisma Role-Model Exercise:

Take your favourite aspects of charisma from this chapter and make note of how you would like to be when it's your turn to be in front of others. Think of people you know, famous or family, that have key ingredients mentioned in this chapter on charisma and storytelling. Borrow from them and build your new role model to guide you in getting better at this skill. Questions to ask yourself:

What do they sound like when speaking? (Think volume,

speed, tempo) What does their body language look like? Be specific.

How do they keep audiences listening to them when speaking, telling a joke or story?

Try to adapt these winning characteristics into your joke and storytelling from now on.

See you next time with **Part Eight: In Action – Going Forward in Life!**

Part Eight: In Action – Going Forward in Life

Network Like a Pro – Key Principle

The main philosophy I want to share with you here is to remember that at networking events you have a choice: be a Guest or be The Host (even if you are not actually the true host of the event!) A guest sits waiting for others to take care of them, and a host pro-actively ensures others are having a good time and meets and greets constantly. The host is remembered, and the guest is often not, especially at a large event. You are there for a short time and with a mission – to find and build connections. There is no logical reason to be shy with starting conversations with a smile, and no true reason why you don't have the right to pursue business opportunities through networking. Networking at a networking event is like shooting fish in a barrel – if you are not shy with the trigger. Be the host, by being an active networker. Nothing ventured, nothing gained!

The Elevator Pitch

"Do not say a little in many words but a great deal in a few."

Pythagoras (570 – 495 BC) Greek Philosopher and Mathematician

Do you have a short, 10-second elevator pitch, to easily lead into a longer conversation? To start you off, write down this formula, and then fill it in:

"Hi, I'm (name) and I help (who? Target market) with (what? verb)."

E.g. "Hi, I'm Tom, and I help home-owners update their heating systems to be green and energy efficient."

"Hello, I'm Gina and I help men look sharp in comfortable wardrobes for the office."

"HI I'm Sarah, and I help non-profit businesses develop a cost-effective marketing strategy, both on-line and off."

The idea with this short elevator pitch is to stay focused on the benefit you provide others. You must know who you and your business help. You can choose a different word like aid, assist, support, etc. but if you are stuck, 'help' is a very powerful word.

Here's another structure for the short elevator pitch, to help convey how you or your business can solve the problems/pain points of your target market:

You know how (recurring problem/pain point in industry) ...?

Well, what we do (at ABC Co.) is ...(action) so that ... (pain is relieved).

E.g., "You know how many entrepreneurs lack a solid business background? Well, what we do at YEDI is train entrepreneurs in the most important aspects of business in a short time so that they can run their venture with confidence."

"You know how when you're hungry you don't want to wait for frozen food from your freezer to thaw? Well, what we have developed at IceBlock Co. is a plate made of special material that completely thaws your frozen meat in just 15 minutes. Have you heard of us before?"

There are other formulas for sure. The first one focuses more on telling others about what you do, and the second one on what your business does. Choose the right formula for the right occasion and enjoy the results! Remember to be an active listener as well!

Here are some articles reflecting my early days of networking and some success stories.

Article One: Networking Leads to Free Press for New Entrepreneur – By Ric Phillips

You may be comfortable with the notion of networking, or you may be avoiding it because the fear of it ranks up there with abandonment or public speaking. Let me tell you a personal story about getting free publicity in a popular commuter newspaper, 24

Hours Toronto, through networking.

It was December 2006, and I was attending a networking seminar, hosted by a non-profit organization focused on helping immigrants succeed here in Canada. A friend who was a member had invited me and I wanted to 'go fishing' for communication coaching business, and also, I wanted to see the well-known author/columnist Colleen Clarke who was the guest speaker.

Now for me, this was an early Christmas gift, as I had been reading Colleen's columns for 3 years and incorporating her articles into my coaching/teaching sessions whenever I helped people with their employment skills like cover letters, resumes and interviewing techniques.

During open group discussion at the seminar, I had given my opinion on how immigrants could better enter or deal with the Canadian professional workforce. Simply speaking, I stated that there would always be at least 3 cultures on the table: Canadian, Original or 'Mother' Country, and Corporate Culture. I briefly spoke about the advantages of understanding these 3 different cultures, and how they interact with each other at work.

After the seminar I approached Colleen to buy her book, get it signed, and chat once more, i.e., network! She thanked me for my contribution to the group discussion and took my card. That evening she called me and interviewed me on my views previously mentioned in the seminar, but more expanded. We talked for 20 minutes and had great rapport (I think in part because we are both Leos! □). She wrote about the topic in the upcoming weekly article for the 24 Hours Toronto business section, where she was a regular contributor, (basically giving advice to new Canadians regarding employment, and what to expect from each different culture group) and cited me as a reference complete with my website link. Following that exposure, the non-profit organization itself hired me as a guest speaker for one of their meetings, and I also managed to engage several the group over the years as individual clients or workshop participants.

I felt thankful that my ability to communicate my ideas in the seminar and face to face had paid off with a new, important contact. My story is clear proof that effective professional communication skills are important for networking, for understanding, and for success in business. I was just starting out but did not let that stop me from achieving goals in networking. The free publicity and work really helped my young business. My advice remains "nothing ventured, nothing gained."

Article Two: Networking Leads to Free National Media Coverage of Political Debate – By Ric Phillips

I am currently a recognized body language expert. Let me tell you how I got really recognized for this unique communication skill.

In 2010 I was contacted by a book publisher who had a client releasing a book called "Winning Body Language" and was asked if I would like to read the book, and possibly allow a blog post or two on the book to be published, to help spread the word during its release. The publisher found me because I had already written a few articles and blog posts regarding body language and non-verbal communication, and I was an established Communication Coach in the city. It made sense to me to pass on a recommendation for the book, if it was good, and I was truly honoured to help.

The book was mailed to me and after I read it, I contacted the publisher and let her know that I indeed did enjoy the book and would be happy to endorse. I was then contacted by the author, Mark Bowden, who had a prepared press release article that would give some quick body language tips while at the same time expose readers to his new book, and the relevant links. Mark was extremely gracious and polite, and I felt immediately comfortable with him, just through email. We exchanged a couple of emails as we went about putting up his articles on my sites, and one thing led to another, and one of us suggested meeting up for a coffee and chat.

I met Mark and we had a lovely conversation about communication, body language, presentation skills, and different business models. I suppose one would expect this when two people meet up who are so well versed in rapport-building skills, but you never know until the meeting, do you? It went so well that to show you the reader just how comfortable I was with Mark, I informed him gently that his book had a few of spelling/grammar mistakes in it and gave him the printed-out list. He laughed and thanked me, and he reviewed the misprints then and there, and agreed with my suggested edits. He told me that this book had already gone through a professional editor or two and joked that he should get me to edit the next book for him. It was all in good fun and he autographed my book, and we parted ways.

Not too long after that I was contacted by Mark as some media outlets had contacted him requesting radio interviews for the upcoming 2011 federal government leadership debates. Mark could not grant the interview requests as he had a conflict of interest – one of the leaders, Prime Minister Stephen Harper, was his client. Because of our long conversation over coffee that day, Mark knew that I could step up and give proper analysis and commentary on the leadership debate. Mark also kindly offered to compare notes after the debate finished airing, so that I could be even more prepared for the upcoming interviews.

I did two radio interviews the next day, one for Vancouver and one for Toronto, and that led to a call from a local TV station, CP24, who were interested in body language analysis of the leaders during their debate. I prepared video clips for them and went on the air live the next day and got about 9 minutes of one-on-one interviewing time with the host, Stephen LeDrew. This free publicity was gold, and it led to other media interview requests for upcoming political debates, celebrity interviews, and reality TV clips. I then put that video up on my YouTube channel to further milk it!

I still get requests today for body language analysis or public speaking commentary, and I must think that at least part of the reason is because I have established credibility and proven ‘likability’ on media outlets. This means reporters can tell from previous interviews if I would be a fit for their story, and what kind of commentary I can provide.

Mark and I keep in touch and collaborate often, and I hope the friendship continues. But just imagine if I was shy about networking, or couldn't see the value in meeting the author of a new book, or couldn't clearly express to Mark my own communication skills and expertise? What if I had let that opportunity slip away?

Article Three: In Action – Top 10 Tips for Effective, Stress-Free Networking – By Ric Phillips

Networking is telling people who you are, what you do and why they should care, without it sounding like you are hard selling yourself or your business directly. It is relationship building.

To be successful at networking first you cannot allow yourself to be a wallflower. Here are my personal tips for success at a networking function so that you can be prepared (which will help combat any anxiety you may have about going and meeting strangers) and come off looking and sounding smooth and successful.

1. At home, write out a list of your personal strengths, attributes, special skills, etc. so that you know why someone should be interested in you as a person and as a professional. Next make the same list regarding your business and its products or services. Now these strengths are in your head, front of mind, to boost your confidence and remind yourself of why people should talk to you or listen to you, whether you are discussing yourself or your business.

2. Visualize the room; visualize smiling, shaking hands, talking to people, exchanging ideas, asking questions, exchanging cards, etc. Visualization works well, especially for shyer people, and many successful people in business, sports, entertainment etc. use visualization to get an image of a successful action before going out to the event.

Visualization gives the brain a pathway to successful outcomes. It really works.

3. Show up with confident posture, a controlled medium-paced walk, a genuine smile and a firm-but-fair handshake and make lots of eye contact.

4. Use the immediate environment to get the conversation started, like talking about the venue, the host, etc. and then find a common bond to keep the small talk going. For example, talk about different networking functions you have attended, or talk about any common interests regarding sports, current affairs, vacations, hobbies etc. Small talk at first is normal and expected, before you get down to business.

5. Now, have questions prepared to ask, to get people to talk about their needs, and then shape your conversation to reflect how you or your services could help in those areas. Don't be pushy. Soft sell yourself. Build interest. For example, instead of saying: *"I sell office insurance…do you happen to need some?"* you might instead

say: "Do you have your own office? Do you feel the insurance premium is a bit high or not? I'm just wondering if you are getting the best value for your money because I'm in the industry, and I help business owners become aware of the fair market value of office insurance." Now they are more ready to be "helped" by you.

6 Remember to repeat their name back to them, actively listen, and keep a mental/physical database of some details of the person with whom you are speaking to. This will come in handy when you re-connect.

7 Always collect a business card or exchange information on your cell phones if possible, and feel free to be the first one to ask for it. Ask with some enthusiasm and at the time when he or she has just talked about what they do or how they can help you (*assuming you are genuinely interested in pursuing this connection.*) Smile and offer yours. Ideally, if you are talking about yourself correctly, people will ask you for your card. However, if they don't, you may choose to offer it.

8 When you go home, write out information on the back of the card or on a sheet of paper, stapled to the card, or of course on your computer. These details help build and maintain rapport for the next and subsequent meetings, emails, and phone calls. Everyone appreciates being remembered!

9 Email them within 3 days to say that it was nice to meet them, and perhaps mention a detail you remember, and suggest you both 'keep in touch'. Don't be afraid to 'be the first' to contact others. That is a powerful leadership impression.

10 Unless you had already planned a meeting previously, follow up a week later and see if you can arrange a drop-by visit or a coffee, if you think the relationship has potential. Once again it is okay to initiate contact if you see the value in the relationship.

Article Four: How to Network at Your Holiday Schmooze Fest – By Colleen Clarke

The holiday schmoozing season is upon us. If you are working on a reputation or would change the one you have, these meeting and greeting tips might be helpful as you attend parties and social/business gatherings.

Check out the dress code beforehand and dress appropriately. Either way, look like a million bucks. Follow these guidelines and you'll make a positive lasting impression:

- Wear your nametag on the right side or at mid chest level in the centre. We usually shake hands heart to heart, so it is easiest to read someone's tag when placed on the right. Bending over to read your nametag at belly button level is just not acceptable.
- Stop at the doorway before you enter and scope out the room.
- Enter a room with confidence and look for someone you know or someone else standing alone. Approaching people who are alone guarantees you a friend for life, if not the rest of the night.
- Most people head for the bar or food table first. This is an easy place to initiate conversations. Eat only consumable food unless garbage receptacles are evident and handy.
- Always have and bring professional looking business cards whether you are employed in a profession or a trade, or unemployed.
- Ask for other peoples' business cards, and then offer yours at the end of the conversation if you really want them to have it and they haven't asked for it.
- Have an opening line prepared to engage an individual. This can be in the form of an opening statement or open-ended question.
- Inquire about people's interest in attending the function.
- Don't take up too much time with one person -- five to seven minutes is the suggested length of time per person. Mingle and spread yourself around.

- If you announce you are leaving, leave.
- Thank the host or organizer of the event before you leave.

Colleen Clarke (www.ColleenClarke.com) is a career specialist and corporate trainer and author of "Networking -- How To Build Relationships That Count" and "Work in Progress."

BONUS – Video where Colleen Clarke answers the question "What is a Corporate Trainer?" on NCCA Canada YouTube channel here:

https://www.youtube.com/watch?v=nDsHAA28xyQ

I hope these stories and articles have inspired you to network like a pro!

Reviewing Online Profiles for Business or Social Connections

If you are a client of mine and wish to get feedback on your social media or business profiles, I'm happy to review them and let you know what I think. I look for impact, emotional content, consistency of messaging, and if your intended message is coming across accurately. If you are not a client of mine, you may still use these criteria and ask a trusted friend to do the same evaluation. A fresh set of eyes offers unique insight. □

Here's a resource article on this subject you may find useful:

http://theundercoverrecruiter.com/write-professional-bio-social-media/

Book Summary:

The art of small talk is about making a good first impression and making others comfortable with you, hopefully even interested, so that you can move from small talk to 'big' talk. Going deeper into conversation is where the relationship building happens, but you've got to start somewhere, and that's the point of small talk skills. First impressions have a very long life, so we must be careful how we start off with new people. Following the tips and techniques based on the theories presented in this book will give you a deep understanding of this interpersonal dance and give you an edge when building your network. I hope you have enjoyed this topic too. Life is short – go meet some people.

Your Communication Coach,

Ric Phillips

Founder, President, Head Coach & Trainer

3V Communications Ltd.

Toronto, Ontario, Canada

https://3vcommunications.ca/

Additional References and Recommended Resources

BOOKS:

First Impressions: What You Don't Know About How Others See You by Ann Demarais and Valerie White.

How to Win Friends & Influence People by Dale Carnegie.

Irresistible Attraction: Secrets of Personal Magnetism by Kevin Hogan & Mary Lee LaBay.

Networking: How to Build Relationships that Count by Colleen S. Clarke.

Talk Your Way to the Top: Communication Secrets to Change Your Life by Kevin Hogan.

Tapping the Iceberg: Achieve Straight A's in Life Through Attitude, Aptitude and Action by Tim Cork.

Winning Body Language: Control the conversation, Command attention, and Convey the right message – without saying a word! by Mark Bowden.

YouTube and Instagram:

https://www.youtube.com/@Charismaoncommand

https://www.youtube.com/@MarkBowden1

https://www.youtube.com/@TheBehaviorPanel

https://www.youtube.com/@joenavarrobehaviorexpert

https://www.youtube.com/@Thedistilledman1

https://www.youtube.com/@RicPhillips

https://www.instagram.com/jefferson_fisher/

https://www.instagram.com/wellwithraele/

https://www.instagram.com/coachricphillips/

www.ingramcontent.com/pod-product-compliance
Lightning Source LLC
LaVergne TN
LVHW050541100826
845148LV00002B/642